Mousetale

Margaret Gordon

Picture Ladybird

Clarence the cat was cold and hungry.

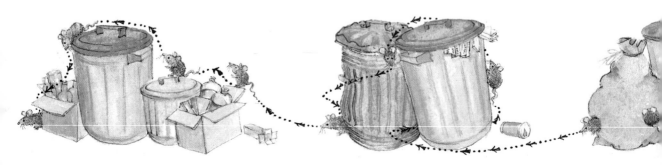

Mirabelle Mouse was cold and hungry.

Mr Spanner was cold and hungry so Mrs Spanner made him a great big breakfast.

Then she packed some cheese sandwiches for him and popped in a surprise cream doughnut.

With breakfast inside him

and sandwiches in his pocket

Mr Spanner drove to work with his usual care,

and arrived safely at his garage. He unlocked
the doors, put his sandwiches on the table and
got to work.

Clarence the cat and Mirabelle Mouse also got to work.

After a while Mr Spanner felt hungry.

He looked at his watch.

 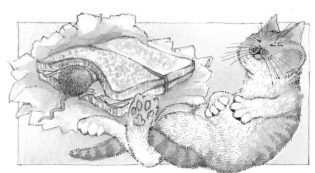

He reached for his sandwiches.

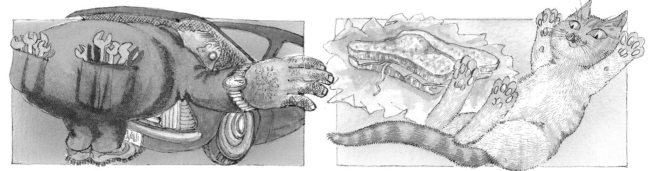

What??

A cat was nibbling the sardines and a mouse was chewing the cheese! Mr Spanner grabbed at the cat

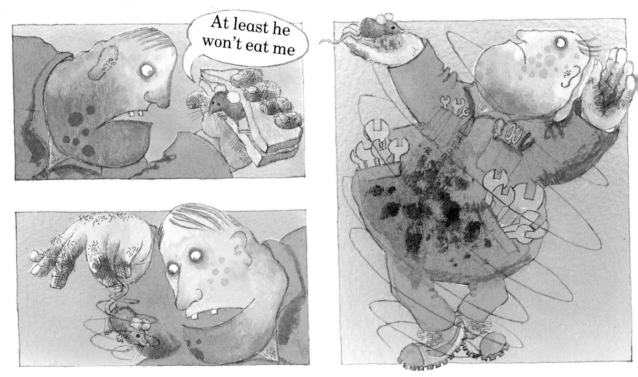

and caught the mouse. He turned a nasty red colour, and then an even nastier green.

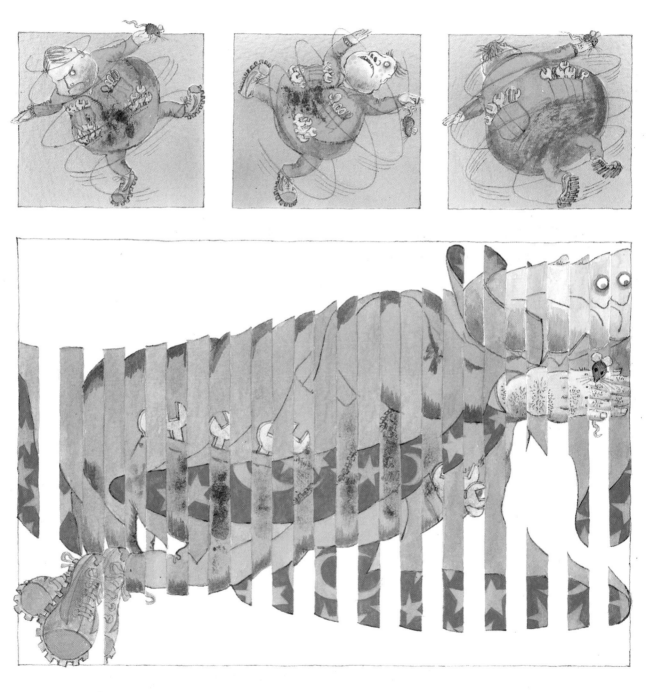

Mr Spanner slowly spun round.

Faster and faster he went,

until he had spun himself into a wizard.
He waved his magic wand and put a terrible
spell on Mirabelle Mouse.

Mr Spanner sat down. He rummaged among his nibbled packages and found Mrs Spanner's surprise cream doughnut. He felt better straightaway and his nasty green glow began to fade.

Mirabelle Mouse, however, was in a dreadful fix. Her tail grew longer and longer and longer and longer.

She was almost glad when the cat bounded back for more sardine sandwiches.

Clarence looked at Mirabelle's tail. "Better not go back for more sardine sandwiches," he said. He looked again at Mirabelle. "If I could get rid of that mousetail she'd make a lovely dinner," he thought. "Why not help her lose it?"

So the cat and the mouse went for a little walk

to have a little think about what to do. This
was a mistake.

The mousetail got into lots of dreadful muddles.

"Little mouse," said the cat, "this is a dog's life. We must go back to Mr Spanner, and ask him to undo his spell."

And so with some difficulty they retraced their steps,

and came back to Mr Spanner's garage.
Mr Spanner was busy.
Mr Spanner wouldn't help.
Mr Spanner hadn't a minute to spare.
It was almost time to go home for his tea.

Mirabelle Mouse sat down on a pair of pliers and began to cry.

"Cheer up," whispered Clarence, "I think I can make Mr Spanner change his mind."

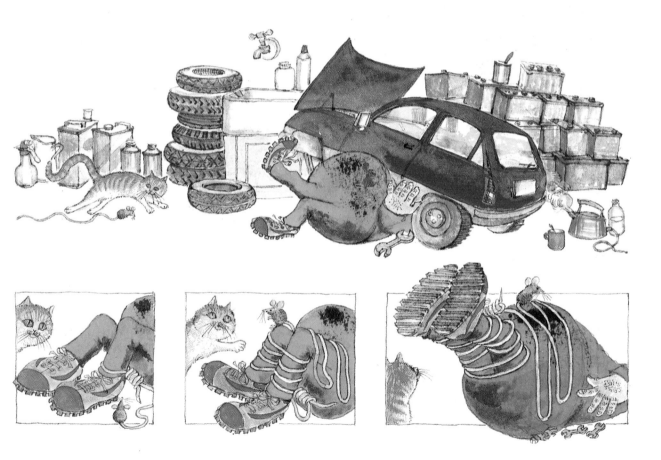

At five o'clock Mrs Spanner wondered why
Mr Spanner had not come home for his tea.

At ten past five she went to look for him.

Mrs Spanner drove with her usual care, and

arrived safely at the garage. She was amazed to
find Mr Spanner tied up in a parcel!

Mr Spanner,
whatever are
you doing?

Mr Spanner was unhappy. He didn't like
Mrs Spanner seeing him tied up in a parcel.

He was fed up with cats and mice and mousetails.
"All right," he said, and glowed green. "I'll undo it."

He said the magic words. There was a puff of pink smoke and a flash of blue light.

"How's that?" he said to Mrs Spanner. Mirabelle's extra-long tail had vanished.

Clarence the cat and Mirabelle skipped away.
It felt wonderful to have a mouse-sized tail again.
To celebrate they went to Signor Minestrone's
café and had a large plate of spaghetti with a
bottle of Chianti.

They went to the pantomime to see "Cinderella",

Mirabelle Mouse looked at Clarence the cat. He didn't look nearly so friendly.

The clock began to strike twelve. Mirabelle slipped quietly away before the day turned into tomorrow.

and then, still feeling rather full, they played hide-and-seek in the little park next to the church.

The church clock said it was almost midnight. The day was nearly over.

Clarence the cat looked at Mirabelle Mouse. How sleek and fat she was. Tomorrow she would be a most sustaining breakfast.